PLAYING

Sunaina Ali

Art by Debasmita Dasgupta

I can Sing

सा.. रे.. गा.. मा..

I

can

Swing

I can play any game!

I can Giggle

I can Wriggle

Everyone Shouts my Name!

AYESHA
आयेशा
आयेशा
AYESHA

I can Race

I

can

Chase

I

can

Count in tens.

I can't

walk

But
I
RO

OCK

for
I have
lots of
FRIENDS.

FRIENDS
FOREVER

THINK

What is your favourite game?

Despite all the odds, Ayesha can do all the things that she wants to do.

Think of a challenging situation that you have been in.

How did you feel?

What did you do?

Were you able to get anyone else's support while facing and dealing with the challenge?

ASK

Do you think our country is
fair to people with disabilities?
How often have you noticed children or
teachers with disabilities at your school?
How are they treated?
Anyone can be our friends; classmates,
parents, animals, and even plants!
One of Ayesha's friends was a bird.
Who is your friend?
Draw a picture of your friend.

DISCUSS

How can we have more people
with disabilities taking part in
different fields, such as sports,
teaching, politics, medicine, arts
and other walks of life?
Discuss the ways in which we
can make that possible in our
country.

ACT

Find out with your friends: how many Children With Special Needs (CWSN) attend your school?

Does your school have options, such as, ramps and elevators along with stairs that everyone can use?

Do all children get equal support while playing sports?

Are Children With Special Needs encouraged to participate in Extra-Curricular activities?

Write a letter to your Principal requesting him/her to include more provisions in the school that can be used by everyone.

Ayesha shows us that if we have the will power, a sense of joy and the ability to laugh – we can achieve many things that are important to us. What do you want to achieve in life? Make a list of these things.

For each item on your list – include what kind of action you need to practise to achieve your dreams.

ACHIEVE

FRIENDS FOREVER

Sunaina Ali loves reading. She also likes to draw and write.

Debasmita Dasgupta does social campaigns for non-profit organisations. She loves illustrating for children's books and has a special interest in cinema, theatre and music. Currently, she resides in Singapore.

KATHA

ISBN 978-81-950681-1-1

Our Mission: Every child reading well for fun and meaning!

KATHA is a registered nonprofit organization started in 1988. We work in the literacy to literature continuum. Devoted to enhancing the joys of reading amongst children and adults, we work with more than 1,00,000 children in poverty, to bring them to grade-level reading through quality books and interventions.

A3, Sarvodaya Enclave, Sri Aurobindo Marg, New Delhi 110 017

Phone: 4141 6600 . 4182 9998 . 2652 1752

E-mail: marketing@katha.org, Website: www.katha.org, www.books.katha.org

Ten per cent of sales proceeds from this book will support the quality education of children studying in Katha schools.
Katha regularly plants trees to replace the wood used in the making of its books.